DO NOT

To my parents, Mel and LaVonne
(with apologies for my nocturnal habits) —R. V. S.

For my beautiful wife (and sleep expert), Natalie —M. B.

Published by Roaring Brook Press
Roaring Brook Press is a division of Holtzbrinck Publishing Holdings Limited Partnership
120 Broadway, New York, NY 10271 • mackids.com

ISBN 978-1-250-21830-8
Library of Congress Control Number 2020919581

Our books may be purchased in bulk for promotional, educational, or business use. Please contact your local bookseller or the Macmillan Corporate and Premium Sales Department at (800) 221-7945 ext. 5442 or by email at MacmillanSpecialMarkets@macmillan.com.

First edition, 2021 • Book design by Aurora Parlagreco
The illustrations in this book were created digitally.
Printed in China by Hung Hing Off-set Printing Co. Ltd., Heshan City, Guangdong Province
10 9 8 7 6 5 4 3 2 1

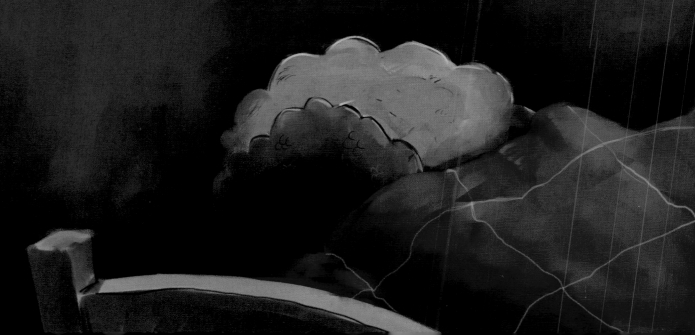

Good Night, Alligator

REBECCA VAN SLYKE   illustrated by **MIKE BOLDT**

Roaring Brook Press

New York

Alligators
do NOT
stop playing and
go to bed.

Alligators are
nocturnal, and
nocturnal animals
don't go to bed when
it gets dark.

They stay awake and play.

All.   Night.

Long.

Alligators don't take showers.

They don't like it when the shampoo bubbles drip down into their yellow eyes.

It stings.

Alligators take baths in the swamp instead, where they can splash around and sink all the boats.

Put your pajamas on, alligator.

Alligators
don't wear
pajamas.

The bottoms get tangled up, and the tops go on backward. Besides, there's no hole for a tail.

But they *might* wear
a nightshirt instead.

A green one.

It takes too long
to brush 80 teeth.

And forget about
flossing.

An alligator *might* let someone help her, though. Only because it's important to keep those 80 teeth shiny and sharp.

Alligators don't go to bed, remember?

But if you read a story about sharks or crocodiles or grizzly bears, they *might* listen to it. Just to get tips on how to be fierce.

Let's tuck you in, alligator.

Alligators don't **want** the covers tucked in.

They need space to roll around and around and thrash their powerful tails.

Alligators *could* lurk just under the surface
to hunt their prey.

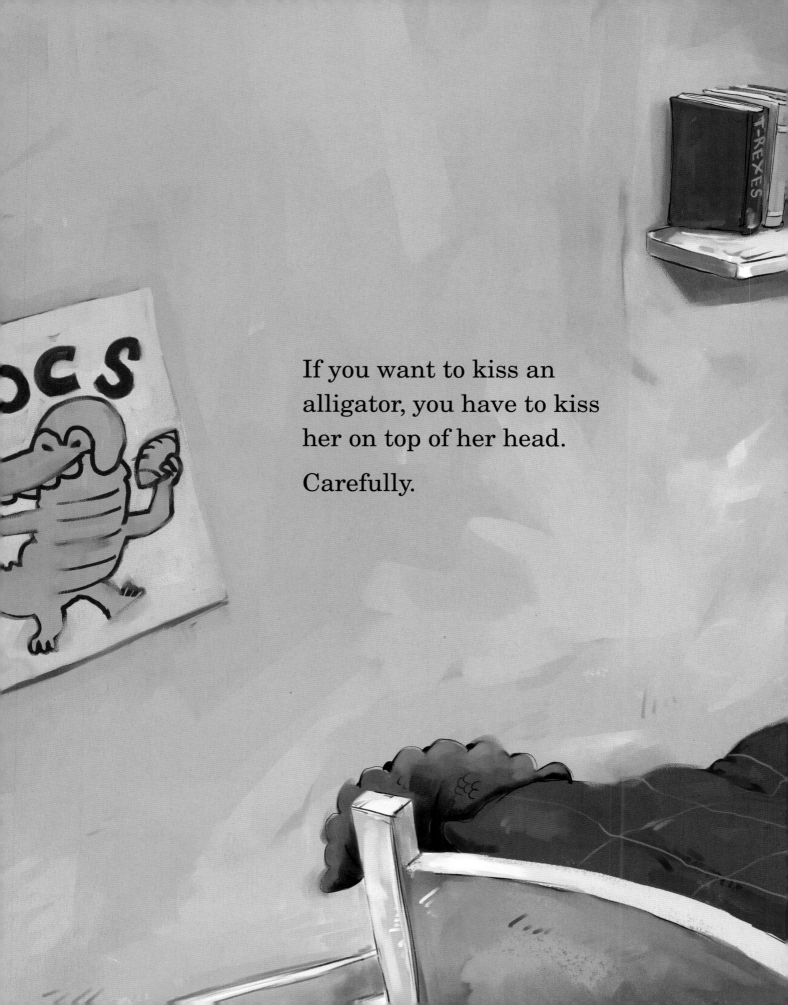

If you want to kiss an
alligator, you have to kiss
her on top of her head.

Carefully.

Lights off, alligator.

Alligators do **not** want the light turned off.

Why?

It's not because they're afraid
of the dark. They're not.

Really.

It's because alligators
are nocturnal.

Alligators . . .

do not . . .

go . . . to . . .

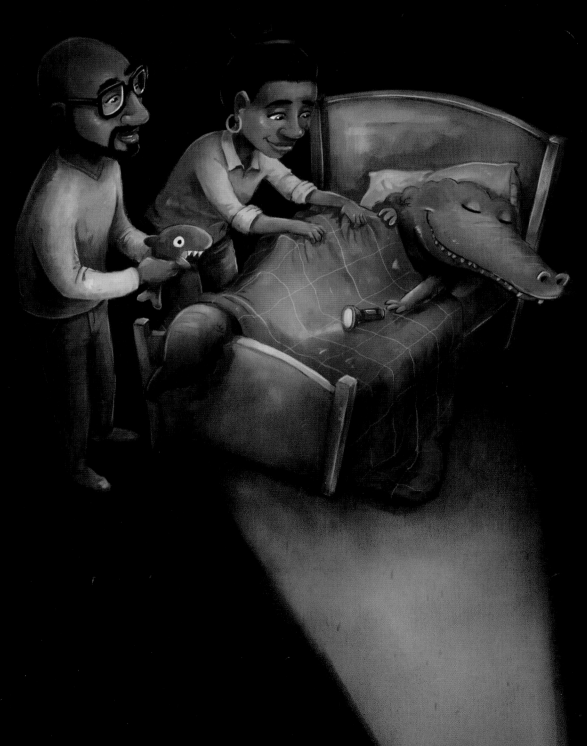

bed.

ALLIGATORS

- Go to bed!
- Put away toys
- Take showers
- Brush Teeth